ICE, ICE, PUGGY

Adapted by **SARA MILLER**

Based on the episode by **DARRIN ROSE**
For the series created by **HARLAND WILLIAMS**

Illustrated by the **DISNEY STORYBOOK ART TEAM**

Los Angeles • New York

First Paperback Edition, September 2017   10 9 8 7 6 5 4 3 2 1
ISBN 978-1-368-01031-3
FAC-029261-17209
Library of Congress Control Number: 2017942130

Printed in the United States of America
For more Disney Press fun, visit www.disneybooks.com

SUSTAINABLE FORESTRY INITIATIVE
Certified Sourcing
www.sfiprogram.org
SFI-01415

Bob comes inside.
Bingo and Rolly run to greet him.

Bob wants some iced tea.

"Oh, no!" Bob says. "No more ice!"

Bob is sad. Iced tea with no ice is just plain old tea. Bob goes to work.

"We need to find ice for Bob,"
says Bingo.

"A.R.F. can help," says A.R.F.
He shows them a picture of Antarctica.
It is at the bottom of the earth.

Antarctica has lots of ice.

"Cool," says Rolly.
"You mean cold," says A.R.F.
"Let's go!" says Bingo.

Bingo and Rolly race to the airport.
They find a plane to Antarctica.

The pugs make it to Antarctica.
Now they need to find the best ice.

"WHOOAAA!" Bingo and Rolly slip
and slide on the ice.

They slide into a penguin. "What are you two doggies doing here?" he asks.

"We need to find the best ice!"
says Bingo.
"If you watch my egg, I will find you
the best ice," says the papa penguin.

"Just keep my egg off the ice till it
hatches," the penguin says.
The pugs agree.

Just then, it starts to snow.
The wind starts to blow.
The puppies can't see a thing!

When the storm ends, Mr. Penguin
is gone.
Bingo and Rolly will keep his egg
off the ice.

Suddenly, the wind blows the egg away!
The puppies slip and slide after it.

The egg slides into an icy cave.
Bingo and Rolly slide into the cave, too.

The pups catch up to the egg.
It is broken! The baby penguin hatched!

"We should go find Mr. Penguin," Rolly says.

The baby penguin waddles away!
"Come back," calls Bingo.

Suddenly, the icy cave begins to crack!
Huge icicles fall all around them.
The icicles form an icy maze.
"We gotta get out of here!" shouts Rolly.

Bingo runs this way. Rolly runs that way. At last, they find the way out!

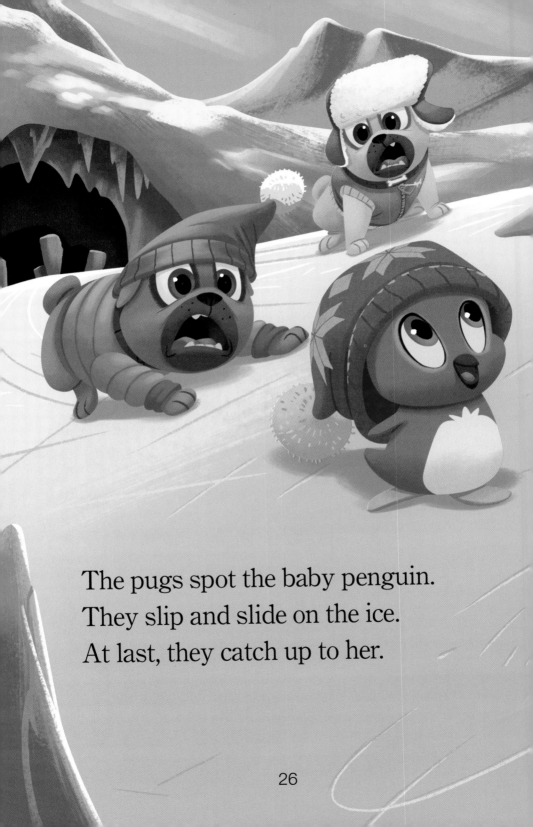

The pugs spot the baby penguin.
They slip and slide on the ice.
At last, they catch up to her.

Then they hear a CRACK!
The ice under them breaks off
and floats away!

The ice starts to sink.
"This ice isn't floaty enough to
hold us!" says Bingo.
Then they hear a voice.

It is Mr. Penguin! "I have your ice.
Do you have my egg?" he asks.
"Da-da!" says the baby penguin.
"My little girl!" says Mr. Penguin.

The pugs put the ice in their collars.
They wave goodbye to their friends.
Then they head for home.

Bob comes home. His glass is full of ice for his iced tea! "Now where on earth did that come from?" he asks.